Sid the Fiddler and the Coastal Critters

written by Doreen Baumann • illustrated by Kate Fallahee

To our younger readers: Here are a few words you will learn:

crustacean (krus-tay-shan) a crab, lobster, shrimp, or barnacle
decapod (dek-a-pod) having ten walking legs, including claws
estuary (es-tu-ar-y) when freshwater meets the saltwater area
petroleum (pet-ro-lee-um) gasoline made from crude oil

First Printing, 2021

ISBN: 978-1-7362675-0-9 paperback
ISBN: 978-1-7362675-1-6 hardback

Follow the Coastal Critter Chronicles at
www.doreenbaumann.com

Illustrated by Kate Fallahee
Edited by Krista Zimonick

Thank you ASB for new beginnings and for encouraging me. DSB

Special thanks to the following for their assistance:

Sally Murphy, retired SC Department of Natural Resources biologist who
started, and ran for 30 years, the state sea turtle conservation program;
Dawn Brut, Curator of Education at the Coastal Discovery Museum,
a Smithsonian Affiliate on Hilton Head Island, South Carolina;
and Michaela Johnson Yates, Bluffton Elementary School Counselor
and Master Naturalist from the Lowcountry Institute.

"Not a care in this island paradise,"
laughs Sid the Fiddler as he is relaxing
and sipping his smoothie while swinging
in the South Carolina Lowcountry.

"On a breezy summer day, the sun is shining,
and by the ocean, my critter friends are frolicking."

Smart and sturdy Daisy the Marsh Tacky,
a rare breed of a pony is running
with Maud the Sporting Dog, her voice baying,
while chasing a ball in a hurry.

Rey the Osprey, a raptor—a bird of prey,
is doing aerial displays.

Finn the Dolphin is breaching, doing flips, and diving.

Sharon the Great Blue Heron with her neck so lightning-fast
spears a small crustacean in the tall marsh grass.

Mildred the Loggerhead, a sea turtle mother,
finds a nesting spot, then uses her flippers
to dig in the sand dunes about eighteen inches
to deposit her eggs for soon-to-be-born hatchlings.

In the estuary, Skip the Shrimp, a decapod crustacean,
is doing flips from the shrimp trawler in slow motion.

Beulah the Blue Crab, a crustacean with a prickly disposition,
quick to use her two sharp front pincers,
swims among a group of crab pots.

And Quinn the Diamondback Terrapin, one sweet lady,
the only turtle to live in salt marsh estuaries,
is swimming without flippers,
only clawed webbed feet to power her forward.

Tom the Red Drum, a redfish with his
air bladder muscles vibrating,
makes musical sounds of drumming
while he feeds on crabs, shrimp, and other small fishes,
vacuuming the bottom in the marsh grasses.

Living in the intertidal reef,
Joyce the Oyster, a bivalve mollusk,
squirts water through her gills to feed and to breathe
as she improves the water quality.

As humans come to town in their trucks and SUVs,
their luggage racks are loaded, ready for the beaches.
With bicycles, chairs, tents, sun umbrellas, and coolers,
they bring plastic pails, shovels, and other belongings.

Moms and dads, brothers and sisters
set up their tents with their blankets and coolers.
Kids build moats around sandcastles,
and some ride with their carts and bicycles.

While others launch their boats
and start up their propellers,
some make ready their cast nets
and load soda in their coolers.

Then one evening, humans gather for a celebration.
They let go of hundreds of balloons filled with helium
tied with colorful plastic ribbons
and watch them float over the ocean.

Every night, more trash is left behind by the visitors.
As time passes, the piles of plastic rise.
The sun breaks it down into tiny pieces,
and beachfront houses have their blaring lights on.

Then one day, a high tide washes
the trash into the ocean.
The plastic plates, bags, and shovels
float along the ocean surface.

As Mildred the Loggerhead
swims ashore with her eggs to deposit,
she gets herself tangled up
in the balloon plastic ribbons.

Then the Loggerhead hatchlings
follow the bright house lights away from the ocean
as they begin to spin around in a commotion.

Then some little Loggerhead tykes
fall into tire tracks left by the bikes.

Quinn the Diamondback Terrapin
gets herself caught in
an abandoned cast net.

The leaking motor oil, spilled by the boat owners, covers the tiny shorebirds with slimy ooze on their feathers.

Over time, the cooler of white foam,
made from petroleum,
breaks into millions of small pieces
and causes chaos, as it looks like popcorn
to the fishes that see them.

"Calling all Critters.
Come to the rescue.
Our island paradise
is in a crisis!"
Sid the Fiddler cries.

Quickly, Beulah the Blue Crab
uses her sharp pincers
to cut the balloon strings
tangled around Mildred's head.

In a mad dash, Rey the Osprey
picks up the balloons and plastic bags
that look like jellyfish
and even tiny black shreds
from the bike tire treads
with the spikey scales on his toes.

Using her special feathers,
Sharon the Great Blue Heron
goes into overdrive
to save the tiny shorebirds
that are struggling to stay alive.

Then turning to Quinn the Diamondback Terrapin,
who is about to drown,
Beulah and Sid cut the cast net
around her neck, so tightly wound.

Finn the Dolphin activates
his sonar-sounding system
to locate objects on the sea bottom.

Skip the Shrimp uses his panoramic eyes
and whiskers to gather all the tiny plastics.
Then he flips them backward into a bucket
that looks like a duck, but
is now full of shovels and junk.

Suddenly, seeing the Loggerheads' spinning motions,
Beulah and Sid use their pincers
to hold up blankets in front of house windows,
so the hatchlings can follow the moonlight
to find their way to the ocean.

Maud the Sporting Dog
helps the hatchling Loggerheads
by using her hind paws
to cover up the bike tracks.

While sliding on her side and paddling,
Daisy the Marsh Tacky pony
gathers the popup tents, chairs, and umbrellas
and anything else she finds unhealthy.

Joyce the Oyster and her brothers and sisters
help to clean the water that went out of kilter,
as they each can daily filter fifty gallons of water.

And Tom the Red Drum
and his fish friends with their tails up
clean the sea bottom with their mouths down.

"Our visitors pack their bags
without their popup tents and plastic stuff,
unaware how our lives were touched,"
sobs Sid the Fiddler, looking crushed.

"What can we do to prevent this again?"
they all cry out in unison.
"How can we keep our island paradise
a clean environment for our locals and
all our visitors and a safe ecosystem
for us coastal critters?"

"What if we make friendly signs and post them on the beaches?" suggests Skip the Shrimp.

"I know!" shouts Sid the Fiddler, "Let's make signs that say it all: **Please Keep OUR Home Clean and Safe** and put all our pictures on them."

What can YOU do to help the Critters?

- Reduce, Reuse and Recycle your plastics;
- Don't release balloons outside anywhere;
- Pick up your pet's waste;
- Join a cleanup of your beaches and waterways;
- Dispose of your trash correctly;
- Don't abandon crab pots or fishing gear;
- Fill beach holes and knock over sandcastles;
- Be a more careful boat owner;
- Cover beachfront lights at night during turtle nesting season;
- Leave the critter alone and observe from a distance; and
- Don't feed the wildlife.

Which one of the Coastal Critters is described on each page?

The answers are found at the bottom upside down.

I live in the salt marsh pluff mudflats
between the high and low tide marks.
I have one small claw for eating
and one big one that I use like a fiddle.
I wave my big claw up and down
to attract a mate or fight a little,
but if I lose it, I can grow a new one when I molt.

With my walking legs, I dig a hole in the mud called a *burrow*.
I climb inside and plug the hole when the tide rises;
I come out to feed when the tide recedes.
Or when it's cold, I stay inside through the winter season.

I shovel mud into my mouth with my claws,
filtering out the edible algae, fungus, and microbes.
I leave sediment balls on the top of my burrow:
the larger dark balls are made from tunneling;
light-colored balls remain from eating.

My female mate remains inside the burrow
during the two-week incubation period
and then comes out to release her eggs,
which are swept out to sea by the tides.

What am I?

a) Great Blue Heron

b) Fiddler Crab

c) Osprey

d) Shrimp

For the younger folk to keep it fun,
read until they guess the correct one,
then move on.

b) Fiddler Crab

I am a bivalve mollusk.
That means I have two shells connected with a hinge.
One shell is cupped and the other flat but often tilted up.
I am handpicked off the banks by pickers in the river
and brought back to the docks to be opened by the shuckers.
I provide employment for local workers
and a nutritious food source for thousands of humans,
as well as many other predators.

I live with others in a cluster called a *bed* or a *reef*
along the coast in the bays and estuaries.
I provide a habitat for many marine species.
I can produce up to one hundred million eggs annually.
In the water column, my larvae float freely
until I become *spat* when I attach myself
to other shells eventually.

I filter water through my gills to feed and breathe,
improving the water quality and clarity significantly.
My friends and I promote the growth of underwater grasses
and serve as essential habitat for other species.
Humans create new reefs through restoration
by returning our shells to the estuaries after we are eaten.

What am I?

a) Marsh Tacky

b) Dolphin

c) Blue Crab

d) Oyster

d) Oyster

I am a decapod crustacean with ten walking legs
and ten swimmerets on my segmented abdomen.
With a swimming type of locomotion,
I can use my tail to flip backward.

I have two pairs of antennae or whiskers,
that allow me to have feelings and senses.
With compound eyes and panoramic vision,
I detect any movement, which protects me
from predators within my surroundings.

My friends and I often live in schools near the sea bottom
along the coasts and estuaries, as well as in rivers.
We are caught in cast nets
and by large fishing boats called *trawlers*
from May through December in South Carolina.

What am I?

a) Dolphin

b) Oyster

c) Shrimp

d) Sporting Dog

c) Shrimp

I am a rare breed of a pony
found only in the South Carolina territory.
I am an herbivore mammal with four hooves.
I am small in size and measured at my withers,
using your hand for every four inches.

I once roamed freely by the hundreds
through the coastal Sea Islands.
Now there are only about four hundred.

I was brought to the Sea Islands and coastal regions
by Spanish explorers, settlers, and traders
as early as the 1500s.

I am sturdy and smart, and I thrive in challenging surroundings,
such as lowland swamps and water, without panicking.
Often used for cattle herding and wild game hunting,
my ancestors served as pack animals for Native Americans
or carried goods back to colonial markets like Charleston.

My breed was used in battle by the legendary Francis Marion,
nicknamed the "Swamp Fox" during the American Revolution.
After the Civil War, we were used commonly
by members of the Gullah community,
transporting children to school,
plowing fields, or even doing mail delivery.

What am I?

a) Marsh Tacky

b) Great Blue Heron

c) Blue Crab

d) Red Drum

a) Marsh Tacky

I am a canine carnivore that is a favorite of humans.
Originally bred from wolves,
I am known for my speed and a keen sense for hunting.
I come in many different breeds
with coats that are coarse to woolly,
short or long, straight, smooth, or even curly.
Our tails may be like a corkscrew, straight, curled, or even pointy.
I have whiskers on my chin to detect objects,
often in the dark and subtle vibrations.
I detect forty times more scents than our human friends
and rapidly pinpoint sounds in the right direction.

At hunt clubs, my kind can help our human companions
as we point to, flush out, and retrieve game that has fallen.
We began hunting for food and protection twenty thousand years ago.
Then came fox hunting as a formal activity,
which originated in England in the sixteenth century.

With my loud voice and scenting ability,
I can chase a quarry with great agility.
Field members wearing formal attire
and "colors" to show seniority
ride on horses called *hunters*
until the fox goes to ground very quickly.
Englishman Robert Brooke was the first to bring his pack
to America in 1650.
Former Presidents George Washington and Thomas Jefferson
kept packs of my kind before
and after the American Revolution.

What am I?

a) Loggerhead Turtle

b) Sporting Dog

c) Marsh Tacky

d) Oyster

I am a raptor—a bird of prey.
Often called a fish hawk or sea eagle,
I am brown above, white below, and look very regal.
With a white head and brown mask around my eyes mostly,
my feathers are water repellant and oily.
I live near water along coastlines, lakes, and estuaries,
as I am the only hawk to feed on fish exclusively.

I keep to open areas, flying with stiff wingbeats
with a steady, rowing motion of my six-foot wings.
Circling the water high above,
I use powerful wings to stop and hover,
then plunge, talons first, into the water
to pick up a fish three feet under.
Then up like a wet dog, I shake, and I shudder.
Moving one of my three front toes to the rear,
I carry my fish with its head forward,
one foot in front of the other.

I choose one mate, sometimes for life, when I am four or three.
I build a nest of piles of sticks in open surroundings
in the tops of trees or even poles for utilities.
Then my lady mate collects the leaves
before she lays her eggs of two or three.

We do high aerial displays called "sky dancing,"
often reaching six hundred feet in elevation.
Then we dive down to the nest, wings drawn in tightly,
with a fish in our talons while screaming.

What am I?

a) Osprey

b) Fiddler Crab

c) Great Blue Heron

d) Diamondback
Terrapin

a) Osprey

I am a coastal treasure,
a wading bird, and a beautiful example of nature.
Typically, my kind is seen along coastlines and in marshes.
We rarely venture far from bodies of water
but are occasionally seen flying over upland areas.

With very slow wingbeats, tucked-in neck, and trailing legs,
we weigh about five pounds, thanks to our hollow bones.
Our six-foot wingspan makes a joy to see in flight
as we fly up to thirty miles per hour as we glide.

We build stick nests, mostly high off the ground,
but sometimes in shrubs near the water's edge,
where we gather in colonies called *rookeries*,
often on islands far from our enemies.
In spring, we return to the colonies,
where females lay two to six pale blue eggs,
which both parents protect and incubate.

Standing up to forty inches tall vertically,
I have a long S-shaped neck vertebrae
and a wide, dark stripe over my eyes.
My plumage is violet and blueish gray
with patches of *powder down* on my belly
to prevent me from becoming slimy and oily
after wading around in the marsh all day.

My long black legs entice fish in shallow waters,
while I wade and probe with long, deliberate steps.
Then, with a lightning-fast thrust of my neck,
I spear the fish or small crustacean,
often swallowing it whole, using my good night vision.

What am I?

a) Dolphin

b) Marsh Tacky

c) Great Blue
   Heron

d) Osprey

I am a large sea turtle with an oversize head.
My descendants probably lived about 120 million years ago.
With four powerful flippers, my kind swims through the world's oceans.
My top shell *carapace* is reddish-brown,
over thirty-six inches when fully grown.
My bottom shell, or *plastron*, is pale yellow.
Each serves as external armor,
although I cannot retract my head
or flippers into the interior.
My beak-shaped mouth and powerful jaws can crush my prey,
as I feed on bottom-dwelling invertebrates,
such as gastropods, bivalves and decapods, and even sponges.

Nesting usually occurs between the May to August season.
I exit the water and climb high up on the beaches
to the top of sand dunes or near the dune grasses.
I use my strong flippers to make a cavity of about eighteen inches.
There, about one clutch of 120 eggs I deposit.
I lay four to six clutches about two weeks apart.
Without seeing my hatchlings, to the sea, I depart.
Then hatchlings are born from July through October.
Sadly, only one hatchling in a thousand matures.

After thirty years swimming the oceans,
females who leave their home beaches as hatchlings
return to nest in the same coastal regions
where they were born, using a unique sense of navigation.

Don't pick up or carry the hatchlings,
you might interrupt their "sense" of direction.

What am I?

a) Diamondback Terrapin

b) Osprey

c) Red Drum

d) Loggerhead Turtle

I am a marine mammal known for my intelligence.
I can live up to fifty years in temperate and tropical oceans.
Called a bottlenose for our short snouts and curved mouths,
I am dark gray on my back and light gray on my edges.
I breathe through a *blowhole* at the top of my head
because, for only about seven minutes, I can hold my breath.

I live mostly alone or in groups of two to three;
sometimes I gather in *pods* temporarily.
Our unique way of hunting is called *strand feeding*.
At low tide, we herd our prey onto steep, smooth muddy banks
of shallow backwater creeks
and push a batch of fish onto the shore for our feast.

Males mate with multiple females annually,
but females only mate every two to three years, typically.
Calves are often born in the spring and summer annually,
and females raise them and bear all the responsibility.

I propel myself by moving my *flukes*, or tail fins, vertically,
while I use my two side flippers for steering mainly.
My dorsal fin on my back, I use for stability
and to prevent me from spinning laterally.

I leap above the water surface frequently,
as jumping causes less friction and saves energy.
This type of traveling is known as *porpoising*;
sometimes I flip up twenty feet, called *breaching*.
I use a type of sonar system called *echolocation*
to locate and identify objects or perceive distance and direction.
With clicks and whistles and other vocalizations,
I communicate with individuals as a form of identification.

What am I?

a) Diamondback Terrapin

b) Dolphin

c) Shrimp

d) Red Drum

I am a vertebrate with scales and gills.
I am one of the three most popular inshore species,
along with trout and flounder fishes,
from the Gulf of Mexico to Massachusetts.
As adults, we average eight pounds and a length of thirty inches,
but we can grow to four feet and weigh on average fifty pounds.

With a whitish belly and coppery red on my back,
the large black eyespots on my tail distinguish me
to make my predators attack the wrong end of my body
and give me a chance to escape from my enemies.

I suck fiddler crabs out of their burrows by *tailing*.
By waving my tail with my mouth downcast,
I vacuum the bottom in the tall marsh grass.

Coming near shorelines from late summer to fall season,
we spawn in estuaries and along barrier island beaches.
Males attract females with sounds of knocking or drumming
that are made with their air bladder muscles vibrating.

Females lay millions of eggs, and in twenty-four hours,
currents carry these larvae to shallow waters
to feed on *detritus*, or decomposing plant and animal matter.

What am I?

a) Red Drum

b) Blue Crab

c) Loggerhead
Turtle

d) Great Blue
Heron

a) Red Drum

I have ten legs and am called a decapod crustacean.
A bottom-dwelling omnivore with a prickly disposition,
I am quick to use my two sharp front pincers.
Due to my fifth pair of legs, called *paddles*,
my scientific name means "beautiful, savory swimmer."

My shell, or *carapace*, is an olive-greenish color.
Males have bright blue pincers and claws.
Females have red on the tips of their pincers.
When I am cooked, I turn a red color.

Male and female gender can be determined
by the shape of their belly or *apron*.
Males have an inverted "T" that is pointy and long.
Adult female's apron is broad and round,
while younger females are triangular.

Our mating season stretches from May to October.
Males mate several times, but females only once a lifetime.
As many as two million eggs, or a *sponge*,
develop in the female's apron.
In about two weeks, the eggs are released into the waters
and carried in currents out into the ocean.
There, the larvae molt and make their way back to the estuaries
to restart their reproductive activities.

As early as the 1600s, we were important food items
for European settlers and Native Americans.
Now we are caught in wire mesh box traps.
Please only keep males that are at least five inches across the carapace,
and release the females so they can procreate.

What am I?

a) Sporting Dog

b) Shrimp

c) Blue Crab

d) Fiddler Crab

I am the only turtle to live in estuaries
and salt marshes on the Atlantic and Gulf coastlines.
My skin is gray to whitish with black spots and squiggles.
I am named for my diamond-patterned shapes
called *scutes* (scoots) on my top shell, or *carapace*.

Males have shells reaching five inches—females are larger at nine—
and we can live thirty years or longer in the wild.
We have salt glands around our eyes
that allow us to survive in changing salinities,
but we require fresh water for drinking.
So...I have a special capability
to obtain fresh water successfully.
I can drink the freshwater rain layer separately,
and with my mouth, I can catch raindrops orally.

I live in cordgrass marshes at high tide
and often burrow in mudflats at low tide and night.
I am a strong swimmer, but I have no flippers,
only webbed feet that power me forward.

Adults mate in the early spring, and by the early summer,
females lay clutches of four to eight eggs,
often from more than one father.
After sixty to eighty-five days, eggs hatch in summer or early autumn.
In the eighteenth century, we became a basic food source;
even the Continental Army ate us.
We were considered a delicacy in the 1900s
and nearly hunted to extinction.

What am I?

a) Great Blue Heron

b) Dolphin

c) Loggerhead Turtle

d) Diamondback Terrapin

ABOUT THE AUTHOR
Doreen Baumann

After graduating from Lake Erie College in Painesville, Ohio, Doreen began a career in managing school textbook production at two New York City publishing companies. Becoming a mother and living overseas took many paths that eventually led to the South Carolina Lowcountry. She enjoys volunteering in local cultural arts, researching history, metal detecting, and visiting state parks in her fifth wheel with her husband, Stu.

The concept for this book began as a kids' tour for her local community that would not only be fun and entertaining but educational. Everything changed in 2020. With experience as a volunteer docent and Marsh Tacky caretaker at the Smithsonian Affiliate's Coastal Discovery Museum on Hilton Head Island, South Carolina, and, after reading about the tons of trash left on the beaches during the summer, the tour became a book with a conservation message.

Contact her at **www.doreenbaumann.com** for activity sheets and more information.

ABOUT THE ILLUSTRATOR
Kate Fallahee

Kate currently works as a freelance children's book illustrator, having worked on multiple books and series, including A Walk With Cooper, I Want an Ostrich, My Shining Star, My Teacher Dad, and The Adventures of Mavis & Margot series. Kate graduated from Northeast Wisconsin Technical College with an Associate Degree in Design & Graphic Technology and now owns her own business, Kate's Illustrations. Her portfolio of work can be viewed at **www.katesillustrations.com**.